Weekly Reader Children's Book Club presents

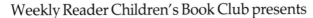

THE SURPRISE PARTY

by Annabelle Prager
pictures by Tomie de Paola

An I AM READING *Book*

Pantheon Books

Text Copyright © 1977 by Annabelle Prager
Illustrations Copyright © 1977 by Tomie de Paola

Library of Congress Cataloging in Publication Data

Prager, Annabelle. The suprise party. SUMMARY: A little boy tries to plan his
own surprise birthday party. [1. Birthdays—Fiction. 2. Parties—Fiction]
I. De Paola, Thomas Anthony. II. Title. PZ7.P8864Su [E] 76-40309
ISBN 0-394-83235-3 ISBN 0-394-93235-8 lb. bdg.

Manufactured in the United States of America 0987654321

To Lucy

who is
full of surprises

CHAPTER ONE

"Know what?" said Nicky.

"No, what?" said Albert.

"My birthday is coming," said Nicky.

"I am going to have
a birthday party."

"Great!" said Albert.

"Are you going to invite me?"

"Of course I am going to invite you,"
said Nicky.

"I'm going to invite you and Ann,
and Jenny and Jan,
and Morris and Doris,
and Dan."

"That sure is a lot of people,"
said Albert.

"You have to have a lot of people
at a birthday party," said Nicky.

"That way you get a lot of presents.
Come on. I need you to help me."

Nicky took out his bank.

He shook it upside down.

Out fell a quarter and two dimes.

"Oh no," he said.

"This is not enough money

for a party."

"What are you going to do?"

said Albert.

"I'll think of something," said Nicky.

Suddenly his face broke into a smile.

"I know," he said. "I'll have a

surprise party."

"A surprise party for who?"

asked Albert.

"A surprise party for me,"

said Nicky.

"You can't give a surprise party
for yourself," said Albert.
"You won't be surprised."
"Of course I can't give
a surprise party for myself,"
said Nicky. "But YOU can.
You and Ann,
and Jenny and Jan,
and Morris and Doris,
and Dan."

"How are we going to do that?"
asked Albert.

"Easy," said Nicky. "You say —

Listen you guys.

Nicky's birthday is coming.

Let's give him a surprise party.

Then they'll say —

What a good idea.

We love surprise parties.

You can bring the cake.

Ann can bring the ice cream.

Jenny can bring the . . ."

"Oh, I get it," said Albert.
"Everyone will bring something
for the party. What a good idea."
"You can get the party ready
at my house while I am out
having my tuba lesson," Nicky said.
"When I come home you will yell,
SURPRISE!
You know, Albert,
I'll be very surprised
if this doesn't turn out to be
the best surprise party that ever was."

CHAPTER TWO

Albert ran home to call up Ann,

and Jenny and Jan,

and Morris and Doris,

and Dan.

Sure enough, they all said,

"What a good idea!

We love surprise parties."

16

They all met at Albert's house
to plan the party.

"We can fix the party
at Nicky's house while he is out
having his tuba lesson," Albert said.
"When he comes home we will jump out
and yell SURPRISE!"
Just then the telephone rang.
Albert answered it.
"Hello," he said.

It was Nicky.

"I forgot to tell you something,"
whispered Nicky.

"I love balloons
with Happy Birthday on them."

"Okay," said Albert, nervously.

"Goodbye."

"Who was that?" asked Ann.

Albert thought very fast.

"Uh . . . that was my Aunt Belinda,"
he said. "Shall we have balloons
with Happy Birthday on them?"

"Yes, yes, yes," shouted everyone.

Ting-a-ling-a-ling.

The phone rang again.

Albert answered it again.

It was Nicky again.

"Can we have snappers?" said Nicky.

"The kind that go bang
when you pull them?"

"Sure, Aunt Belinda," said Albert.

He slammed down the phone
and turned to the group.
"Shall we have snappers?" he asked.
"Do you mean the kind that go bang
when you pull them?" said Jenny.
"They're so scarey. I love them."

Ting-a-ling-a-ling.

"Let me answer it," said Jan.

"No, no, no," cried Albert,

grabbing the phone.

It was Nicky again.

"Be sure that everyone

brings a present," said Nicky.

"And remember

my favorite color is blue."

"Of course, Aunt Belinda," said Albert.

"GOODBYE!"

"Why does your aunt call you every five minutes?" asked Morris and Doris. "My Aunt Belinda is very lonely," said Albert.

"Now let me think.

Nicky's favorite color is blue.

I think I will make

a beautiful blue birthday cake."

"Do we have to bring

a present?" asked Dan.

"Everyone has to bring a present,"

said Albert.

"Oh boy, will Nicky be surprised!"

CHAPTER THREE

The next day Nicky and Albert
were roller skating in the park.
"It would be awful
if anyone found out that I know
about the party!" said Nicky.
"Shush," said Albert.
"Here comes Ann on her pogo stick."
"I'd better make sure
that Ann doesn't think I know
about the party," said Nicky.

Ann stopped hopping.

"Hi," she said.

"Hi, Ann," said Nicky.

"Guess what I am doing on my birthday."

"What?" asked Ann.

She gave Albert a worried look.

"My tuba teacher is taking me

to a concert," said Nicky.

"Oh NO," said Ann.

"Why do you say Oh NO?" asked Nicky.

"Don't you like concerts?"

"What I meant to say," said Ann,

"was, Oh no — no kidding. Excuse me.

I have to go and see Jenny and Jan,

and Morris and Doris,

and Dan."

Ann got on her pogo stick

and hopped away as fast as she could.

Nicky laughed and laughed.

"I fooled her," he said.

"Now nobody can possibly think

that I know about the party.

Oh, I can't wait

for my birthday to come."

CHAPTER FOUR

Three days later Nicky was walking
home from his tuba lesson.
He gave a little skip of excitement
because his birthday had finally come.

When Nicky got to his little house
it was all dark.

He practiced making a surprised face.

He opened his front door.

Nothing happened.

He went into his living room.

Nothing happened.

He turned on the light.

Nobody was there.

"Where's the party?" he wondered.

"Oh, I bet they are hiding."

He waited and waited.

Nothing happened.

Then the doorbell rang.

"There they are!" he thought, happily.

He practiced making more surprised faces

on the way to the door.

It was Albert, all alone.

"Where is my party?" asked Nicky.

"Oh Nicky," said Albert

"It is awful.

Ann told everyone

that you were going to a concert

with your tuba teacher

so they called off the party."

Nicky sat down. "Oh my," he sighed.
"Oh my beautiful surprise party."
A big tear ran down his cheek.
"Don't feel too bad," Albert said.
"They decided to have the party
on your next birthday.
You can look forward to it
for twelve whole months."

"I should never have played a trick
on my friends," cried Nicky.
"Never mind," said Albert.
"I made a cake for you anyway.
Come to my house and we can eat it."

CHAPTER FIVE

They walked to Albert's house.

Albert opened his front door.

Nicky went in.

Albert turned on the light.

"SURPRISE! SURPRISE!"

shouted Ann,

and Jenny and Jan,

and Morris and Doris,

and Dan.

Nicky looked all around him.

There were balloons

with Happy Birthday on them.

There was a table

with a blue paper table cloth

and seven blue paper plates.

By each plate there was a red snapper

and a little basket filled with candy.

Best of all,

there was a pile of presents,

seven of them,

each one tied with a big bow,

and each one with a surprise inside.

"Wow!" breathed Nicky.

"Know what?" said Albert.

"No, what?" said Nicky.

"You said you wanted
the best surprise party that ever was.
So we made it a surprise."

ABOUT THE AUTHOR

Annabelle Prager grew up in New York City. She graduated from Sweet Briar College and then studied at the Yale School of Fine Arts and the Art Students League, and she is an illustrator as well as a writer. THE SURPRISE PARTY was inspired by a birthday party she planned for herself when she was a penniless art student. Her interest in music led her to organize a young people's orchestra in New York City, where she lives with her husband and their two children.

ABOUT THE ARTIST

Tomie de Paola is well-known for the many books he has written and illustrated, including STREGA NONA (A Caldecott Honor Book), CHARLIE NEEDS A CLOAK, and WHEN EVERYONE WAS FAST ASLEEP. He was born in Meriden, Connecticut and graduated from Pratt Institute and California College of Arts and Crafts. He teaches in the visual arts department of New England College and lives in nearby Wilmot Flats, New Hampshire.

Tomie de Paola shares Annabelle Prager's love of birthday parties and says Nicky could just as easily have been him.